MR PATTACAKE

Stephanie Baudet

Sweet Cherry
Publishing

Published by Sweet Cherry Publishing Limited
Unit 36, Vulcan House
Vulcan Road
Leicester, LE5 3EF
United Kingdom

First published in the UK in 2017
ISBN: 978-1-78226-255-8
©Stephanie Baudet 2015
Illustrations ©Creative Books
Illustrated by Joyson Loitongbam

Mr Pattacake and the Skiing Mystery

Wai Man Book Binding (China) Ltd. Kowloon, H.K.

Pattacake, Pattacake, baker's man,
Bake me a cake as fast as you can;
Pat it and prick it and mark it with P,
Put it in the oven for you and for me.

Pattacake, Pattacake, baker's man,
Bake me a cake as fast as you can;
Roll it up, roll it up;
And throw it in a pan!

Pattacake, Pattacake, baker's man.

MR PATTACAKE
and the
SKIING MYSTERY

'Well, *this* will be a different kind of job,' said Mr Pattacake, waving a letter in his hand. 'How exciting!'

He hopped from one foot to the other, doing the usual silly little dance he did when he was excited. It made his big chef's hat wobble, almost falling off his head. Mr Pattacake's hat wobbled a lot. In fact, it wobbled so much that it had become *very* **WOBBLY** indeed!

'But it's not one for you, Treacle. You won't like it.'

That made Treacle, his lazy ginger cat, lift his head from his breakfast bowl.

He was used to Mr Pattacake receiving letters in the post asking him to do different cooking jobs, and he was used to helping the chef, in his own way – like eating up any scraps that found their way onto the floor: sometimes by accident and sometimes not. Mr Pattacake had always said that Treacle was his assistant, so why couldn't he go on *this* job?

'You hate the snow,' said Mr Pattacake, knowingly. 'You tiptoe out when you *have* to go, but you know you hate getting your paws wet and cold.'

Treacle frowned as well as a cat can frown. There *was* no snow! It hadn't snowed since last winter. What was Mr Pattacake talking about?

As usual, Mr Pattacake read his mind. He had been around cats so long that he always knew what they were thinking. At least, that was the case with Treacle anyway.

'I've been asked to cook for a party of children who are going skiing in Switzerland for a week. One of them is having a birthday on the last day too, so there will be a fondue party up the mountain, and then they will all ski down by torchlight. It sounds like a lot of fun!'

Not a lot of this made any sense to Treacle. He didn't know much about skiing and he had no idea what a *fondue* was.

'Skiing is a winter sport,' said Mr Pattacake, lifting up one foot and pointing to it. 'You put skis on your feet and slide down the mountain. And a fondue...' he said, showing off his chef knowledge, 'is melted cheese in which you dip chunks of bread.'

Treacle liked cheese, but he didn't like snow. Nevertheless, there was no way he was going to be left at home on his own, especially with that mischievous tortoiseshell cat, Naughty Tortie, around. She would surely tease Treacle about being left out – she was always jealous of him.

Treacle glared at Mr Pattacake.

Mr Pattacake surrendered.

'It will mean travelling in your cat carrier all the way in the coach,' he said, sighing. 'And you don't like that, either.'

Treacle glared at him again.

'You still want to go? All right then,' said Mr Pattacake with a smile. 'We'll have to make you some little waterproof boots.'

Mr Pattacake sat down with a pen and paper to make a list of the meals he would cook and added an extra little note to himself to find out how to make a fondue. He could buy all the ingredients in Switzerland, but he always liked to have everything planned beforehand. Making lists, he thought, was what made him so good at his job.

On the day before their departure, Mr Pattacake packed a small suitcase for himself and got Treacle's pet carrier down from the loft. Treacle stuck his tongue out and looked at it with distaste, but he knew he would have to travel in it, although goodness knows why he couldn't just sit on a seat like everyone else.

 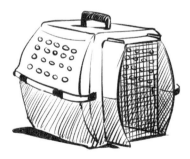

Mr Pattacake had found two pairs of baby shoes in a jumble sale, a pink pair and a blue pair, to stop Treacle's feet from getting cold in the snow. Treacle insisted that the pink ones went on his back feet, where he couldn't see them so easily.

One of the children from the ski party had kindly knitted Treacle a hooded jumper when they had heard that he was coming. It had orange and white stripes and Treacle wasn't sure whether he liked it or not. It felt funny because he wasn't used

to wearing clothes, but he knew how cold it would
be in the mountains. He planned to stay indoors
anyway, in front of a big roaring fire. The jumper
went well with his ginger fur but not so well with
his pink shoes. Mr Pattacake dressed him up and
then showed a very grumpy looking Treacle his
reflection in the mirror. He looked very smart!
(But also a little strange.)

The coach left early. On board was Danny, the birthday boy, and nine other children, plus Danny's parents and four other parents. Mr Pattacake and Treacle sat on the back seat where there was plenty of room.

The children made a great fuss of Treacle, poking their fingers through the holes in the pet carrier. Treacle liked the fuss but he *hated* people poking at him, so he sat there sulking with his head resting on his paw. He was not very happy at all.

'Are you going to ski, Mr Pattacake?' asked Danny.

The chef thought about it for a moment. 'I might give it a try,' he said. 'I'll try anything once.'

No one asked Treacle if he was going to ski.
Even though he didn't want to, he would still have
liked to have been asked.

On the first morning after they arrived, Mr Pattacake hired some skis and followed some of the children to the chairlift. As they set off up the slope, he peered below, watching everyone as they laughed and had fun skiing.

They glided up through a gap in the trees. Suddenly, in the snow below, Mr Pattacake saw some HUGE footprints. He stared at them. What could it be? What kind of animal could have made those? Surely there weren't still bears in these mountains? They didn't look like bears' footprints anyway. They had two round marks in front, followed by two long marks. So it must have been a four-toed creature.

'Look at those footprints!' he said, pointing towards them. But the children in the chair behind were too busy chattering.

Mr Pattacake was worried. All these children were in danger. Perhaps a creature had escaped from a zoo! Oh no!

At the top of the mountain, Mr Pattacake put on his skis ready for his attempt at skiing. In all the excitement, he had almost forgotten about the footprints (although not quite).

Most of the children had skied before and made it look easy. Mr Pattacake pushed off with his sticks, warily.

Now most beginner skiers do a lot of falling down at first, but Mr Pattacake had very good balance, so he didn't fall down at all. The trouble was, however, that he didn't know how to stop!

Skis didn't have brakes, so on and on he went, getting faster and faster, his arms flailing in the air as he screamed.

'**Heeellppp !**' he cried. But no one was able to. All the skiers on the slope just stopped and watched in horror, waiting for a disaster to happen.

Luckily, just before he disappeared into the woods, he ploughed into a huge, soft snowdrift.

SPLAT!

As he stumbled out of the snowdrift, he brushed off as much snow as he could, picked up his skis, which had snapped off in the collision, and began to plod back up the slope. He knew he must look like a walking snowman! Mr Pattacake felt *very* silly indeed.

'Are you all right, Mr Pattacake?' asked one of the children, called Becky.

He nodded. 'No more skiing for me, though,' he said, feeling embarrassed. 'I think I'll stick to cooking.' Then he remembered something.

'Be careful of the monster,' he warned.

Becky looked at him curiously. What could Mr Pattacake be talking about? A monster? Here in the mountains? Surely that wasn't possible.

Mr Pattacake took the chairlift back down the mountain. He was still feeling humiliated, and thought that he should keep his little accident a secret from Treacle – the cat would gloat for sure. When he got back to the ski lodge he expected to find Treacle stretched out in front of the log fire, but he was not there. Neither was he in their room.

Mr Pattacake shrugged. He wasn't too worried about the cat, but it *was* time he began the preparations for the evening dinner. The children and parents would be hungry after all that exercise.

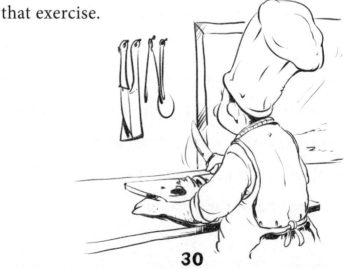

About an hour later, Mr Pattacake received a great shock. He happened to look out of the kitchen window, when a strange sight met his eyes. It was Treacle, dressed in his woolly hooded jumper, zipping past the window riding a snowboard. On his feet were his baby shoes, and someone had even given him a pair of child's goggles. What a peculiar sight!

Treacle expertly jumped off the snowboard and it came to a gentle stop against a tree.

Mr Pattacake stood with his mouth open in surprise. It was still open when Treacle came pattering into the kitchen, looking very smug.

'But… you don't like the snow, Treacle,' said Mr Pattacake, puzzled, staring at the cat in awe.

Treacle pushed off his shoes and tugged at his jumper with his teeth until Mr Pattacake bent down and gave him a helping hand. Treacle shook himself, stretched his paws, and went into the living room to sit by the fire.

'Well,' said Mr Pattacake with a chuckle, his big chef's hat wobbling energetically. 'A snowboarding cat! Who would have thought! But you be careful of that monster out there!'

Treacle frowned slightly, but he was far too cosy to take any notice of what Mr Pattacake had said.

Later, the children and their parents came in, stamping the snow off their boots and putting them near the fire to dry. They all enjoyed the meal Mr Pattacake had made for them, and chattered happily about the exciting day they'd had.

Mr Pattacake told them all about Treacle and the snowboarding, but they just smiled politely at him and then looked at the normal ginger cat sleeping in front of the fire. Mr Pattacake knew they didn't believe him.

Treacle opened one eye and smiled his cat's smile.

There was one thing that puzzled Mr Pattacake, though, over the next few days. He often saw Treacle whizzing past the window on a snowboard, but couldn't figure out how he got it to the top of the slope. Normally people carried them on the chairlift, but Treacle couldn't do that. There were *some* things that were just impossible for a cat.

He decided that before the week was over, he was going to follow Treacle and see how he did it. There was also the fear in the back of his mind that the monster with the big feet would get him. Two mysteries to solve were too much for Mr Pattacake's quick brain. He wanted answers.

But before Mr Pattacake could even begin to investigate, Treacle went missing.

He just didn't come home one evening. It got dark and Mr Pattacake was really worried. He and the children and their parents all went searching, calling out to Treacle as they trudged up the slope.

But all they could hear was silence; they couldn't hear a single sound. As they entered the wooded area, Mr Pattacake looked up at the full moon and wondered again about the monster. But he had to put his fear aside and be brave.

His cat was missing. He cupped his hands to his mouth and called out, '**Treacle !**'

Then all of a sudden, they heard a faint meow coming from further into the trees. They all scrambled through the snow, calling as they went.

The meow was coming from above their heads. Mr Pattacake looked up. There, shivering on the chairlift, stood Treacle. The chairlift was now silent and still.

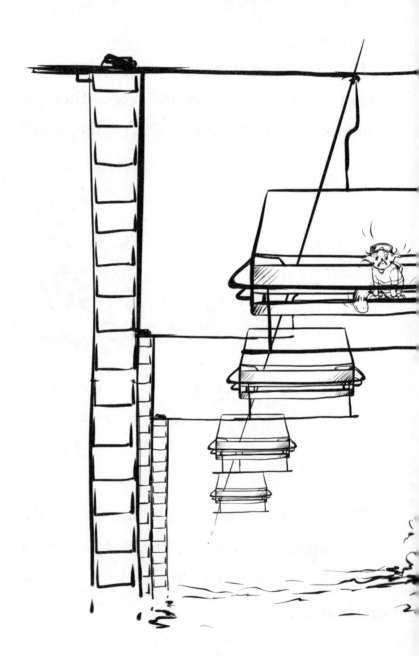

'What's he doing up there?' asked Danny, surprised.

'He must have got on while it was still working and the lift men didn't see him up there,' said his dad. 'Then they must have stopped the lift and gone home, leaving him hanging there.'

Treacle was about four metres above their heads. Mr Pattacake frantically looked around for a solution. Could Treacle jump to the nearest tree? He would have to, otherwise he'd have to wait until the next morning, and it was going to be very cold during the night. Even his hooded jumper wouldn't be enough.

Mr Pattacake pointed at a nearby tree. 'Treacle, you'll have to jump to that tree.' He walked over to it and patted the trunk. 'Come on, Treacle. You can do it!'

'**You can do it, Treacle !**' chorused the children.

But Treacle held up one of his paws. Of course, he had his little shoes on, so his claws were hidden inside. He wouldn't be able to grab the tree with them on.

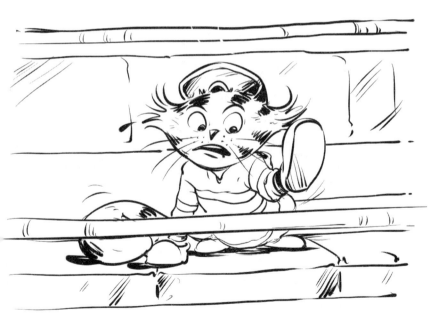

'Take them off, Treacle,' yelled Mr Pattacake, 'and then push them out of the chair!'

As they watched, Treacle tugged and pulled with his teeth and finally got the shoes off. Then he pushed them out and they landed in the soft snow, one by one.

Plop, plop, plop, plop.

Then Treacle stood on the side of the chairlift looking at the tree, trying to judge the distance. His face had a worried expression on it. He sat back on his haunches, ready to spring.

'Come on, Treacle,' chanted the children. Treacle poised, and then jumped.

His claws hooked into the tree trunk and he made his way back down to the ground.

The children cheered. Mr Pattacake sighed with relief and smiled, bending down to pat Treacle. 'Come on, puss. There's a nice meal and a warm fire waiting for you.'

'But why was he on the chairlift in the first place?' asked Becky, who was picking up Treacle's little shoes.

Mr Pattacake was as puzzled as she was. But what bothered him more was how Treacle could snowboard down if he hadn't taken a snowboard up.

The next day was the final day of the holiday, and Mr Pattacake was busy buying food for the fondue and ingredients for the birthday cake he was going to make for Danny. He'd decided on the design of the cake, but he had to bake it first.

After Treacle's adventure on the chairlift the night before, he had spent the morning dozing by the fire, but now he stood up, stretched, and brought Mr Pattacake his hooded jumper and shoes to put on him.

Mr Pattacake thought that, while the cake was baking, he would follow Treacle to see exactly what he was up to.

Treacle strolled down to the bottom of the chairlift where the skiers were getting on. It wasn't too busy, as most people were already up the mountain, so some of the chairs swung by empty. Treacle stood a little way from the start but where the chairs were still quite low to the ground. When the lift man wasn't looking, Treacle suddenly leapt onto an empty chair and was whisked away!

Mr Pattacake hurriedly clambered down to get on a chair himself, but by the time he was on one, Treacle was way ahead of him.

It was quiet and peaceful as he drifted through the trees, but Mr Pattacake couldn't help but look down and search for the big footprints.

There had been a fresh fall of snow during the night and, just as he feared, there was a clear set of footprints right below leading through the trees.

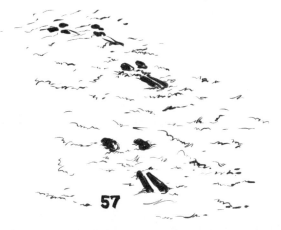

Mr Pattacake shuddered, imagining being there alone with that creature. It was strange that there were no warnings. Perhaps it only came out at night when the skiers were tucked up in their warm beds.

When he reached the top, he jumped off the chair and looked around. Treacle had gotten a good start. What *was* that cat up to?

What he saw next made him gasp, and then grin. Treacle, of course, couldn't carry a snowboard up in the chairlift, so what was he doing? He was stealing someone else's! People who had stopped in the restaurant for a drink or a snack would prop up their snowboards near the ski racks, expecting them to be still there when they came out.

Treacle was now nudging a red snowboard towards the slope, looking round warily in case its owner appeared. When he reached the edge, he gave a little push with one front paw and then leapt aboard just as the snowboard set off downhill.

Mr Pattacake assumed that when he reached the bottom, he left the board and then came back up in the chairlift to steal another one! What a naughty cat! All these people must be wondering how their boards got down the hill on their own!

At least *that* mystery was solved, thought Mr Pattacake as he rode back down in the chairlift. There was still the mystery of the big footprints, but right now, he had a cake to rescue.

He spent the rest of the afternoon decorating the cake and gathering the ingredients for the fondue. As a special extra, he made some chocolate mice, his speciality. He missed Treacle, who was usually there to clean up (eat!) any bits that dropped on the floor. Fancy Treacle preferring snowboarding to eating!

Tonight, after the party, the children were going to ski down in the dark. What fun! Not in complete darkness though – some of the ski lift men would be carrying torches to light the way. Mr Pattacake and a couple of the parents would come down in the chairlift so they could see the children below, skiing down a lit-up piste. It would be a wonderful sight.

A sudden thought came to him. What about that animal? If it was nocturnal, then it may come out while the children were skiing. Would it be afraid of the flame torches or would it be brave and ruthless?

In the late afternoon, Mr Pattacake carried all of the food, including the cake, to the chairlift station, where the man loaded them onto an empty chair. Treacle had finally appeared just before he had left the chalet, so together they climbed onto the next chair as it swung round the great wheel.

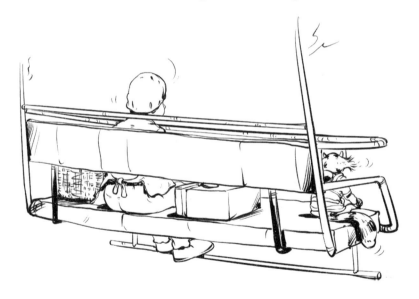

'You missed the chocolate mice,' said Mr Pattacake as he looked below. Treacle turned to look at him, smiling his cat's smile.

'So you've found something better to do, have you? I hope you haven't been getting up to any mischief.'

Treacle gave his best innocent look. Him? In mischief? Mr Pattacake must be getting him mixed up with Naughty Tortie.

At the top, Mr Pattacake carried the box of food to the restaurant where the party was being held.

He left the cake box in a corner at the chairlift station, in case some of the kids tried to sneak a peek.

He then got to work melting the cheese for the fondue and breaking the bread into small pieces, ready to be dipped. He laid out the fondue forks, one for each person, and put the plate of chocolate mice on a shelf as a little treat for afterwards.

By the time the children and adults crowded in excitedly through the door, the cheese was bubbling in each of the fondue pots, which were placed on the burners on each table. A lovely cheesy smell filled the air, making everyone sit down in anticipation.

'Be very careful,' warned Mr Pattacake. 'We don't want any pots knocked over.'

When the last bit of crusty cheese had been lifted from the bottom of the last pot, it was time for the cake, so Mr Pattacake went out to fetch it from the chairlift station.

It was dark outside and very cold. The snow crunched under his heavy boots and his breath puffed out in LITTLE WHITE CLOUDS.

Lifting the cake up carefully, Mr Pattacake made his way back towards the restaurant.

Shivering, he held the cake with two gloved hands, failing to notice the sledge that one of the children had brought up with them. Of course, he accidentally stepped on it.

It zoomed forward and Mr Pattacake was forced to sit down as it slid down the slope.

'Oh **DRIBBLE !**'

Mr Pattacake screamed as the sledge started to move even faster. He was still holding the cake, so he was unable to get out of the sledge. All he could do was sit there as it slid right to the edge of the piste and plunged down onto the smooth frozen slope.

'Help!' shouted Mr Pattacake, but no one could hear him. Everyone was inside the restaurant having too much fun. Treacle, however, looked up, his ears twitching.

Meanwhile, Mr Pattacake was gathering more speed. He tried to stop the sledge by digging his heels in the snow, but it was frozen solid. So down he went, still holding onto the cake. He thought of all that time he'd spent making and decorating it, and Danny, the birthday boy, hadn't even seen it yet. Now it would be smashed to pieces, and he himself was going to have a very unpleasant end to this journey.

Through the trees he went, leaning from side to side, trying to avoid them. There was a full moon, which partly lit his way. Above him the chairs hung still and silent – it looked as if he wouldn't be using them after all.

The air rushing past his face was freezing; luckily, he had put on his woolly hat and gloves to fetch the cake. If he had been wearing his big chef's hat, it would have fallen off by now.

WHOOOOOOSH!

That was close! He just missed that tree!

Whoa! Down he went. Lean over for the bend. Ouch! It was very bumpy and hurt his bottom!

Now he could see the lights of the village below, sparkling in the clear air. He shouted again, but no one could hear, and even if they could, they wouldn't be able to help. How could you stop a speeding sledge with a chef on it, holding a cake ?

THUD! CRASH!

He ploughed into a big snowdrift and stopped at last. Cold snow slithered down his neck and he shivered as he sat in stunned silence, unsure if he was still in one piece. The cake wouldn't still be in one piece though. It couldn't possibly have survived that.

What was he going to do now? The whole party was ruined.

Just then, he heard noises coming from behind him. He twisted his head and saw lights bobbing on the mountainside.

It was the children! They were skiing down by torchlight! Mr Pattacake almost cried with relief. How had they known what had happened to him?

Of course, it must have been Treacle. Cats had a sixth sense. Just as he could read Treacle's mind, Treacle could sense Mr Pattacake's thoughts too.

Or it could have been that cats have hearing that is a hundred times better than a human's, so he may have heard his cry for help.

Good old Treacle!

The bobbing lights got brighter and Mr Pattacake shouted.

'I'm over here!' he called as he waved his hands above his head.

Soon he was surrounded by flaming torches, chattering children, and parents who helped him up out of the snowdrift. One of the ski men had even carried Treacle down as well.

Everyone looked down at the cake box sitting on the snow. There was a hushed silence as Danny's mum carefully opened it.

Inside, the cake, shaped like a mountain, sat intact, without a single crumb broken off. Even the little skiers had managed to stay in place!

A big cheer went up. 'Hurray for Mr Pattacake.
He saved the cake!'

They all went back to the chalet and Danny's mum cut the cake up and handed a piece each to the excited children.

'This tastes delightful after that exhilarating ski down the mountain,' said Danny's dad, with a mouthful of cake.

Before they left the next morning, Mr Pattacake still felt he had to solve the other mystery – the big-footed creature in the woods. He went to the little alpine museum in the village to see what he could find out.

The curator frowned as Mr Pattacake described the footprints.

'We have no big animals here,' he said. 'There are no more bears in this part of Europe, and I can't think of anything else it could be. Could you draw the footprint for me, please?'

When Mr Pattacake did, the curator smiled and nodded.

'That is not *one* footprint, it's *all* of the footprints.'

Mr Pattacake frowned, puzzled.

'They are the marks made by a mountain hare,' said the curator. 'The two round marks in front are the front paws and the long ones behind

are its hind legs. Look, I'll show you one.'

He led Mr Pattacake over to a glass case. Inside he could see the stuffed body of a hare. Its glass eyes stared out from a face which looked vaguely

MOUNTAIN HARE

familiar to Mr Pattacake.

In fact, that hare had the mischievous look of a certain cat – a certain tortoiseshell cat that he and Treacle knew *very* well indeed.

Naughty Tortie!